ICE AGE™
DAWN OF THE DINOSAURS

MY THREE DADS

HarperCollins®, ®, and HarperEntertainment™ are trademarks of HarperCollins Publishers.
Ice Age: Dawn of the Dinosaurs: My Three Dads

For information address HarperCollins Children's Books, a division of HarperCollins Publishers, 10 East 53rd Street, New York, NY 10022.
www.harpercollinschildrens.com
Library of Congress catalog card number: 2009923994
ISBN 978-0-06-168975-8
09 10 11 12 13 UG 10 9 8 7 6 5 4 3 2 1
Typography by Joe Merkel ❖ First Edition

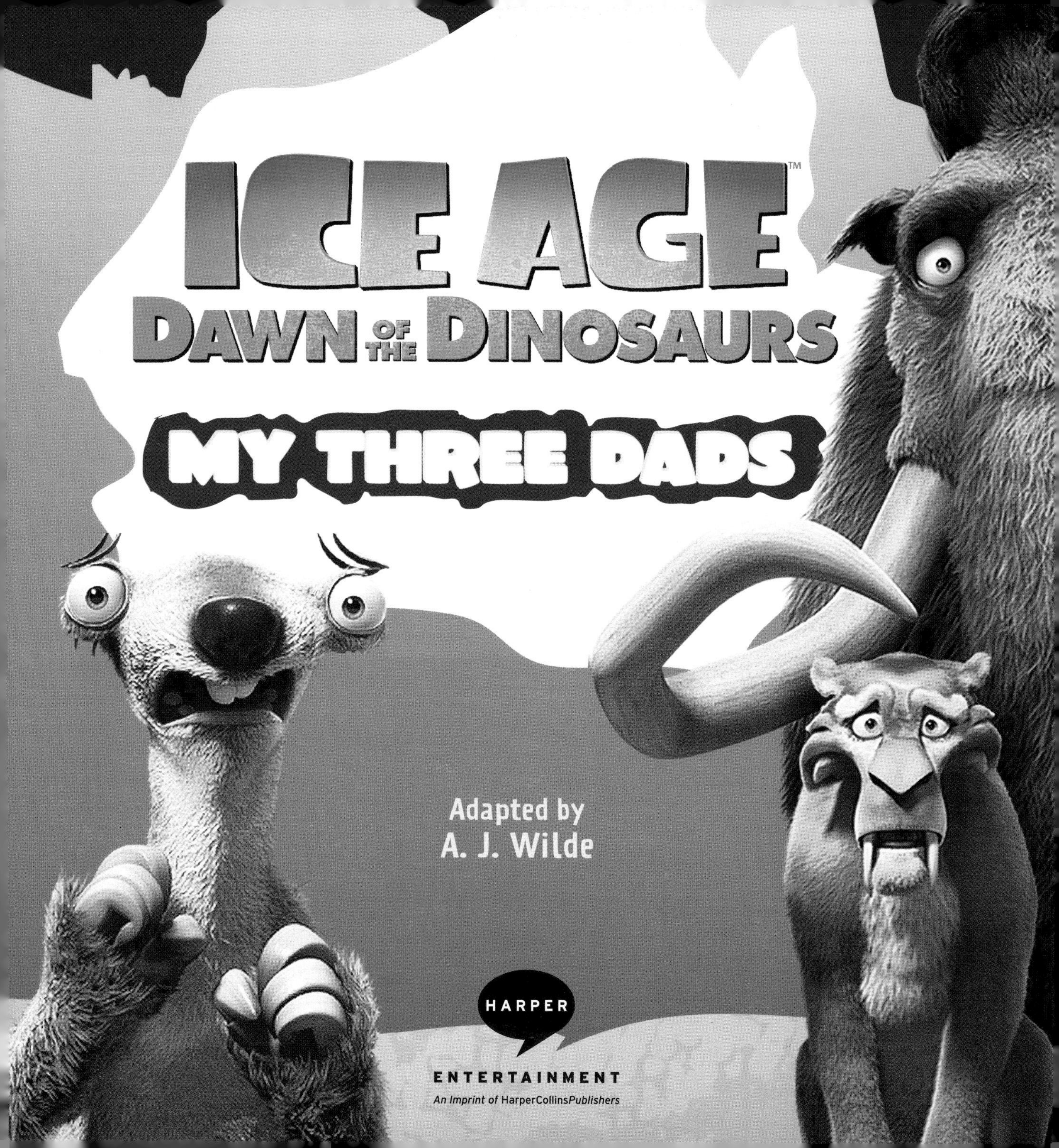
ICE AGE™
DAWN OF THE DINOSAURS
MY THREE DADS
Adapted by
A. J. Wilde
HARPER
ENTERTAINMENT
An Imprint of HarperCollinsPublishers

Manny and Ellie were expecting a baby.

Sid and Diego were as excited as the mammoths for the new addition. They felt like fathers-to-be!

One day, Ellie noticed the pond near the family cave was gone. "Wasn't there a pond over here?" asked a very confused Ellie.

"I drained it," explained Manny. "A baby could drown in a pond!"

"I don't believe it. You're trying to kid-proof nature!" cried Ellie. "Manny, this is the world where our child is going to grow up. You can't change that!"

"Of course I can!" Manny exclaimed. "I'm the biggest thing on earth!"

"Alright, Mister Majestic, good luck with that!" Ellie teased.

Manny formed a plan to make their dangerous world safe for his kid—but he would need help.

As honorary dads, Sid and Diego were behind him all the way.

The three dads were on a mission to make the baby's world as safe and friendly as possible. They set out to change the tundra one piece of frozen danger at a time.

Sid wanted to protect his little buddy from sharp branches! He placed snowballs on their tips.

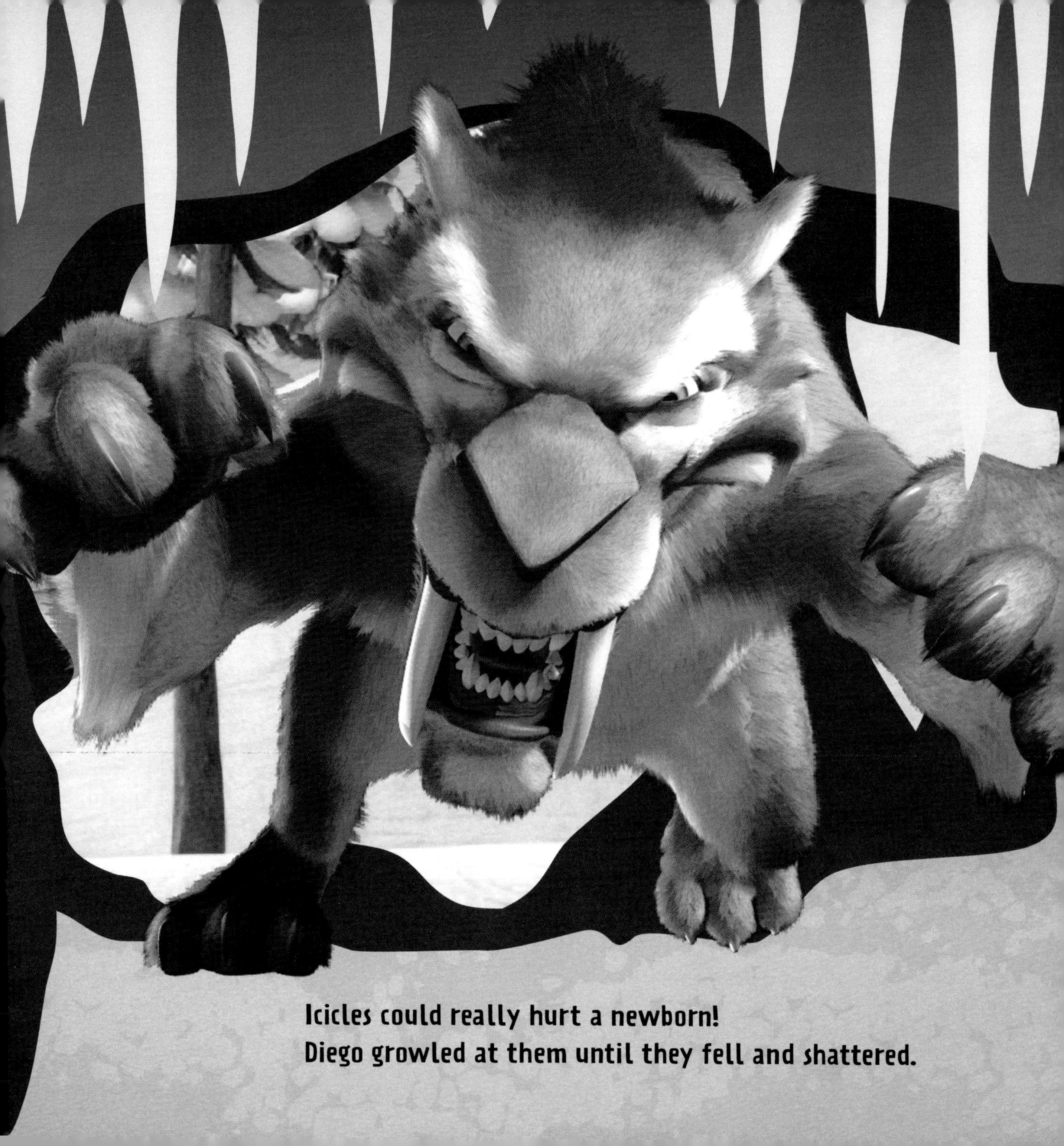

Icicles could really hurt a newborn!
Diego growled at them until they fell and shattered.

Manny didn't want his mini-mammoth to get hurt when learning to walk!
He smoothed sharp rocks over with mud.

When the three "dads" finished with their hard work, Manny showed Ellie what they had accomplished.

"Voila!" Manny yelled.

"Playground for Junior!" Sid declared proudly.

"Oh, Manny. It's . . . amazing! OUCH!" Ellie grabbed her belly.

"What!? Is it happening!?" Manny shouted.

"The baby just kicked," Ellie cried.
"The baby *kicked*?!" Diego exclaimed.
"Are you okay?" Sid asked.
"Yes, and the baby is on its way!" Ellie explained.

Soon enough, baby Peaches was born, and everyone was so excited to meet her. Manny, all of a sudden, worried the ice mobile he made was dangerous. Would it fall on his baby?

"You've got to relax!" exclaimed Ellie. "The best way to protect our child is to have our friends around us."

With extra "dads" like Sid and Diego, the little mammoth would be very safe indeed.